Tumbleweed Stew

Susan Stevens Crummel
Illustrated by Janet Stevens

Green Light Readers
Harcourt, Inc.
San Diego   New York   London

www.harcourt.com

First Green Light Readers edition 2000
Green Light Readers is a registered trademark of Harcourt, Inc.

Library of Congress Cataloging-in-Publication Data
Crummel, Susan Stevens.
Tumbleweed stew/Susan Stevens Crummel; illustrated by Janet Stevens.
—1st Green Light Readers ed.
p. cm.
"Green Light Readers."
Summary: Jack Rabbit tricks the other animals into helping him make a pot of tumbleweed stew.
[1. Rabbits—Fiction. 2. Tricks—Fiction.] I. Stevens, Janet, ill. II. Title.
PZ7.C88845Tu 2000
[E]—dc21 99-50803
ISBN 0-15-202673-8
ISBN 0-15-202628-2 (pb)

A C E G H F D B
A C E G H F D B (pb)

Jack Rabbit opened his eyes. He stretched
and looked up at the pretty blue sky.

Jack's tummy growled. He thought,
The sun is up. The sky is blue!
What a great day for tumbleweed stew!
He hopped along, jumping over brush
and cactus.

Before long, he came to a big gate. Over the gate it said TWO CIRCLE RANCH. Jack slipped under the fence and into a herd of cattle.

"Moo!" said Longhorn. "Move on!"
"Well, howdy," Jack said. "How do you do?
How would you like some tumbleweed stew?"

"There's no such thing as tumbleweed
stew," said Longhorn, munching the
dry grass.

Not a nice place, thought Jack. He ran
down the path to the ranch house.
"Anyone home?" he called.
"*No!*" he heard from inside. "Go away!"
"How about some lunch?" asked Jack.

Armadillo came out onto the porch. "This is my ranch," she said. "This is my food and you can't have any!"

Jack took a chance. He said,
   "But I would like to cook for *you*.
   Have you heard of tumbleweed stew?"
"There's no such thing as tumbleweed stew,"
Armadillo said.

Before Armadillo could blink, Jack started
a fire. He spied an old pot and filled it with
water. He set the pot of water on the fire.
After a while, he stuffed a big tumbleweed
into the pot.

Armadillo looked into the pot. Jack took
a taste and said,
  "It smells so good. It tastes good, too.
    But it needs more, this tumbleweed stew."
"Well," said Armadillo. "There might be some
carrots in my house."

Soon the tumbleweed

and carrots

were cooking
in the big pot.

Buzzard floated down to take a look. "I can smell this food way up in the sky! It needs onions," he said. "I'll fly home and get some."

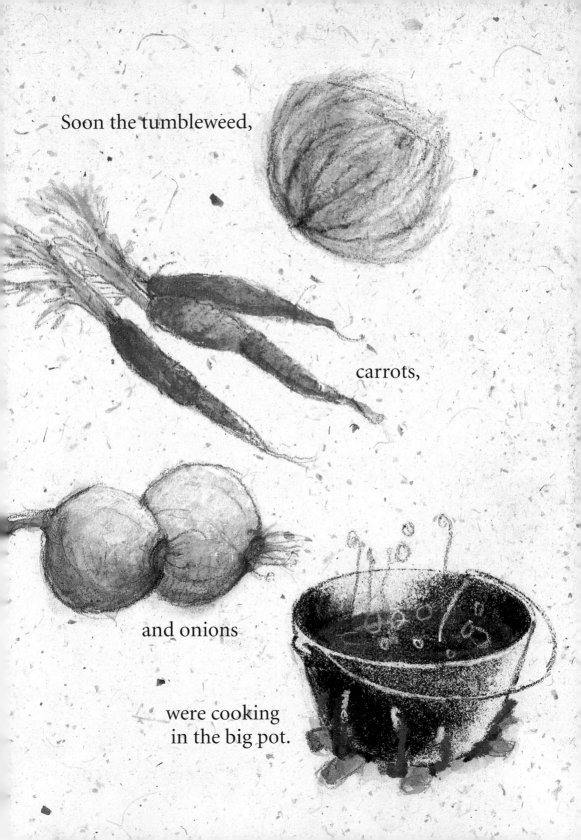

Soon the tumbleweed,

carrots,

and onions

were cooking
in the big pot.

Then Deer trotted over and looked into the pot. "This stew needs corn," he said. "I'll be right back."

Soon the tumbleweed,   carrots,

onions,

and corn

were cooking
in the big pot.

Skunk scampered up to the pot. "Smells good," she said. "But where are the potatoes? I'll go dig some up."

Soon the tumbleweed, carrots,

onions, corn,

and potatoes

were cooking
in the big pot.

Rattlesnake slithered over with some celery. "You can't make stew without celery," he said.

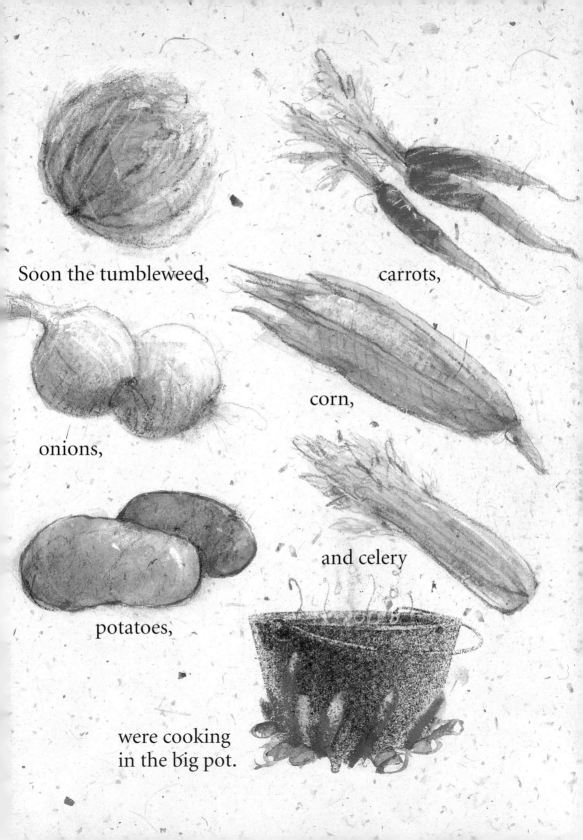

Soon the tumbleweed,

carrots,

corn,

onions,

and celery

potatoes,

were cooking
in the big pot.

Armadillo, Buzzard, Deer, Skunk, and Rattlesnake gathered around the pot of stew. They watched it bubble and steam.

At last Jack cried,
  "It took a while, but thanks to you,
    It's time to eat this tumbleweed stew!"
The animals ate and ate until every bite of
stew was gone.

Armadillo couldn't move. Buzzard couldn't fly.
Deer couldn't trot. Skunk couldn't scamper.
Rattlesnake couldn't slither.
They put their heads down and fell asleep.
Jack slept, too, but not for long.

Jack Rabbit opened his eyes. He stretched
and looked up at the pretty blue sky.
His tummy growled. He thought,
Another day for being sly—
What a great day for cactus pie!

Meet the Author and Illustrator

Susan Stevens Crummel

Janet Stevens

   Susan Stevens Crummel and her sister, Janet Stevens,
grew up in Texas, where Tumbleweed Stew takes place.
The sisters worked together on the story. Susan wanted
the characters in the story to be animals that live in
Texas. Janet kept drawing them until she liked the way
they looked. "The best part of making this story was
working with my sister," says Janet.